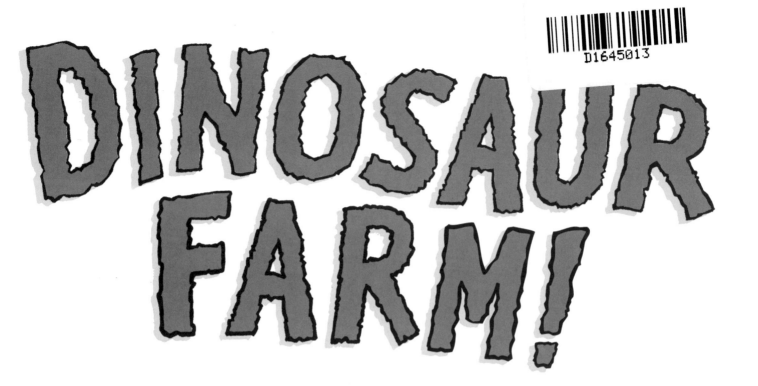

DINOSAUR FARM!

Penny Dale

nosy crow

Farmer dinosaurs working,
working on Dinosaur Farm.

Driver dinosaurs ploughing, ploughing the stony soil.

The stony soil, row after row.

Up and down!
Up and down!
Up and down!

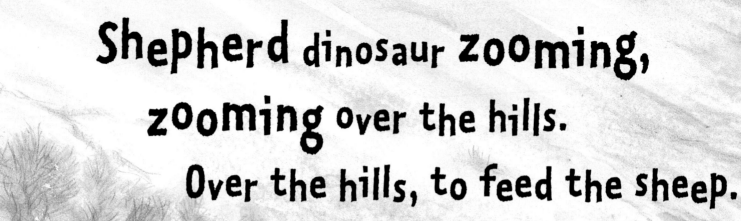

Shepherd dinosaur zooming,
zooming over the hills.
Over the hills, to feed the sheep.

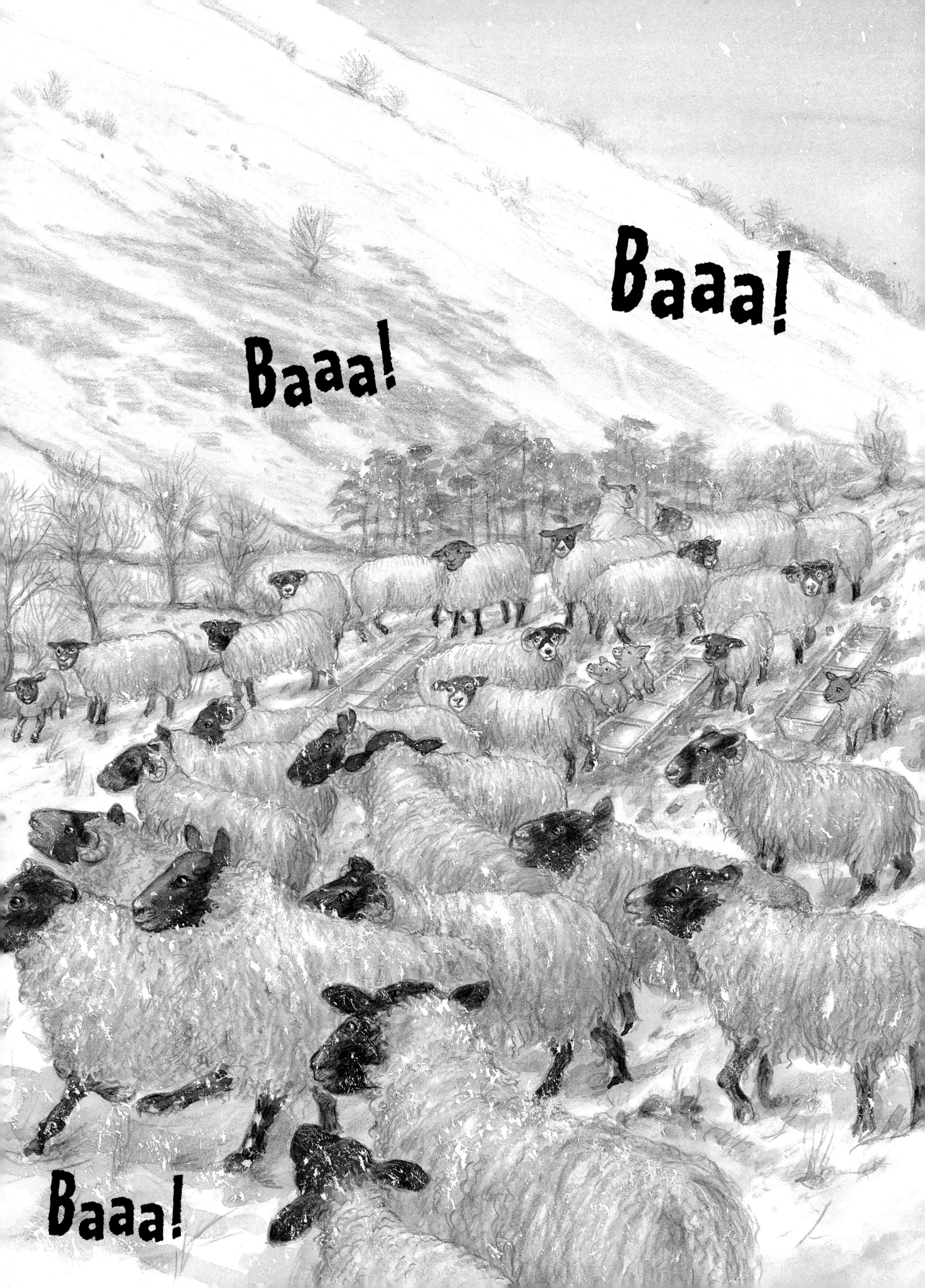
Baaa!
Baaa!
Baaa!

Smelly dinosaur muck-spreading, muck-spreading across the field.

Across the field, feeding the soil.

Splatter!

Splatter!

Splatter!

Haymaking dinosaurs rolling,
rolling up the long grass.
The long grass into giant bales!

Dusty dinosaurs digging,
digging the muddy carrots.

Clatter!

The muddy carrots to be
washed and stacked.
Clatter!
Clatter!

Rumble!

Sunny dinosaurs cutting,
cutting the golden corn.

The golden corn with the
combine harvester.

Rumble!

Rumble!

Climbing dinosaurs picking, picking the juicy red apples.

Excited dinosaurs travelling,
travelling to the **farm show.**

To the farm show with their animals and crops.

Chatter!

Chatter!

Chatter!

Happy dinosaurs cheering, cheering Dinosaur Farm.

Carrot picker

Quad bike

Tractor and plough

Combine harvester

Muck spreader